DATE DUE

DISCARD

Turn this page
to meet characters and
visit places that begin with
the letter H.

What sound does "H" make?

Listen to this story and
soon you will know.

Ready?

Here we go...

To Chet
with love and appreciation
for having the courage
to take this journey with me.
M.T.L.

To Andy
for always
dreaming with me.
To Victoria, A.J. & Alli
for making my
dreams come true.
M.T.S.

To my goddaughter
Elizabeth Genieve
with all my love.
E.M.M.

To the Mary Meuser Memorial Library — Hope you enjoy Hilda's adventure to Hiccup Land! Happy Reading! Marie Rini Tuchetti

Publisher's Cataloging-in-Publication

Tini Sisters.
  How Hilda hushed her hiccups / written by the
Tini sisters ; illustrated by Erin Marie Mauterer.
-- 1st ed.
  p. cm. -- (A letter-sound listen and retell
adventure)
  LCCN: 99-95019
  ISBN: 0-9678459-0-4 (Collector's edition)
  ISBN: 0-9678459-1-2 (Hardcover edition)
  SUMMARY: When Hilda the hyena has a bout of
hiccups, she travels to Hiccup Land for
suggestions, in this rhyming story which
emphasizes the sound of the letter H.

  1. H (The sound)--Juvenile fiction. 2. Hyenas
--Juvenile fiction. 3. Hiccups--Juvenile fiction.
I. Mauterer, Erin, ill. II. Title.

PZ8.3.T56How 2000   [E]
          QBI99-1988

*15 P16
Atori*

Atori™, Read Me Atori™, Letter-Sound™, and Listen and Retell™ along with the trade dress of *How Hilda Hushed Her
Hiccups* are trademarks of the publisher.

Copies of this book and other books in the Letter-Sound™ ◆ Listen and Retell™ Adventure series are available
in bookstores or may be ordered directly from the publisher. Special discounts may apply when books
are purchased in bulk as premiums or for sales promotions or for fund-raising or educational use.
For details, contact Atori Publishing, Inc. • P.O. Box 125 • Olyphant, PA 18447 •
(570) 383-2579 • www.readmeatori.com

Editors: Pam Pollack and Mary Quattlebaum
Copy Editor: Seth Weinstein

10 9 8 7 6 5 4 3 2 1

Printed in Hong Kong

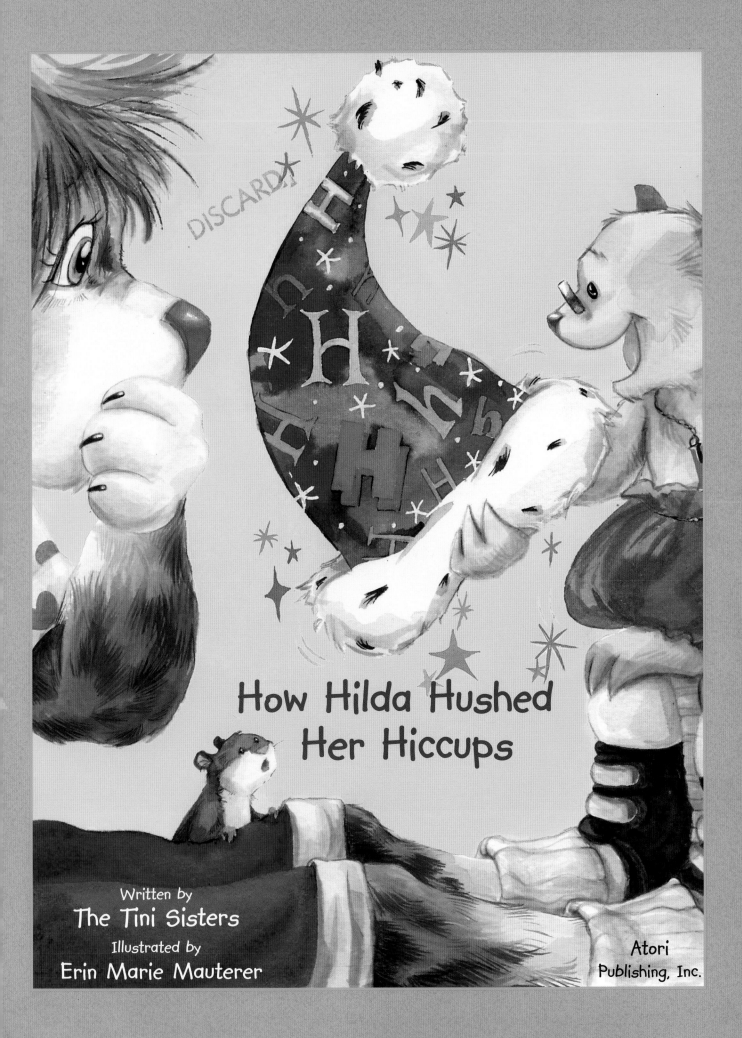

How Hilda Hushed Her Hiccups

Written by
The Tini Sisters

Illustrated by
Erin Marie Mauterer

Atori
Publishing, Inc.

Hilda the hyena had a head full of hair. Hair such as Hilda's was certainly rare. Everyone loved it. Everyone said, "You have the most beautiful hair on your head."

One day, as her hair was being sun-dried, Hilda's body rumbled inside.

Hilda   Harry   Hedgehog

Headband

Hooray

Help

Helicopter

Hopscotch

Helpers

Hay   Horn   Hat   Hill

Hic!

And then something happened.
A hiccup popped out.
Soon hiccups had Hilda
hopping about.

As she hopped and hiccuped
and hiccuped and hopped,
the hyenas around
the Hair Hut just stopped!
"Help me," cried Hilda,
"to stay on the ground!
With these hiccuping hiccups
I hop all around!"

One hyena piped up,
"I know what to do!
Try hopping on one leg
and then hop on two."

"Or this," yelled another.
"Just try something neat.
You could hang upside-down
with your head by your feet!"

"Try holding your breath and then hum a tune!"
"Laugh hee hee and ha ha all afternoon!"

But nothing would take Hilda's hiccups away,

and she hiccuped and hopped for miles that day.

She hopped up a hill that looked very small.
But she hiccuped again and
                        began
                              to
                                 fall.

"**W**hat's this?" she heard
from a huge voice below.
"You're hurting the head
of this happy hippo!"

"Oh, dear," Hilda stammered.
"Forgive me. It's true.
I have hiccups. I'm sorry
for hopping on you!"

"Then go see the Helpers
in Hiccup Land.
The Hiccup Land Helpers
will lend you a hand."

HONK!

So Hilda hopped past
the Hiccuping Hut,
where hot dogs and hamburgers
hiccup somewhat.

Said a hiccuping horse
with a hoof full of hay,
"You'll find Hiccup Land
straight up that way.

"Just hop up that hill.
It's the highest around.
And that's where the
Hiccup Land Helpers are found."

HhHhHhHh

When Hilda arrived
with her hiccuping beat,
the Hiccup Land Helpers
hopped to their feet.
"Hooray! Hooray!" they
sang, hand in hand.
"Everything hiccups
in Hiccup Land!

"But if you don't want your hiccups to stay,
just tell your hiccups to be on their way.
To do this you put on the hiccuping hat.
Say, 'Hush, hush, you hiccups.' Just say it like that."

hush   hush   hush   hush   hush

hush   hush   hush   hush   hush

So Hilda decided she'd give it a try.
She held her breath first, then let out a sigh.
"Hush, hush, you hiccups. Go find a new home.
Hush, hush, you hiccups. Just leave me alone."

And that's when it happened. She no longer hopped.
And then she got quiet. EVERYTHING stopped!

"My hiccups are gone!" Hilda said with a cry,
as she hugged all the Hiccup Land Helpers good-bye.

When Hilda got back
to her happy hometown,
one hundred hyenas
were hopping around.

"Hilda," they cried,
"we have hiccups now, too!"
Hilda then hollered,
"I know what to do!"

Huddled around her,
they hiccuped and hopped,
and Hilda explained
how her hiccups had stopped.

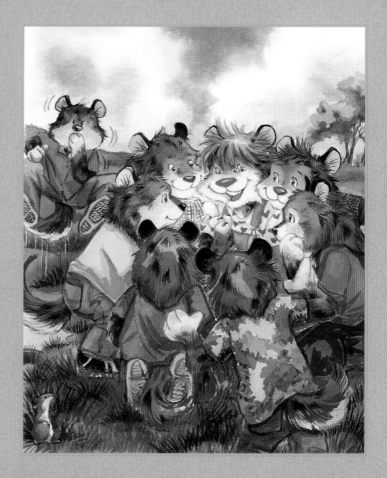

The hyenas hugged Hilda
with hearts that were true.
They sang out in harmony,
"We love you!"

As they held Hilda high,
they yelled, "Hip, hip, hooray!"
And Hilda became
a hero that day!

Now you know the sound that "H" makes.

Listen...

Can you hear the sound?

See if you can tell
someone else the story.

And then
try another
Letter-Sound™ ◆
Listen and Retell™
Adventure.

Retelling Pictures

How Hilda Hushed Her Hiccups

Written by The Tini Sisters

Illustrated by Erin Marie Mauterer

Facts About Hyenas

Have you ever heard someone say, "You're laughing like a hyena"? Well, hyenas are known for the sounds they make that could be mistaken for human laughter. However, hyenas are not really funny. Actually, they're wild and ferocious.

Did you know...

Spotted Hyena

Hyenas live in Africa and Asia.

There are three types of hyenas—the spotted or laughing hyena, the striped hyena, and the brown hyena.

Hyenas have hunched backs because their front legs are longer than their back legs. They have four toes on each foot.

Hyenas are nocturnal, which means they are awake at night. During the night hyenas hunt, and during the day they sleep in caves or holes in the ground.

The striped hyenas and the brown hyenas are endangered. That means they are in danger of disappearing from Earth.

To find out more about hyenas, look in an encyclopedia, visit a library or a museum, or try surfing on the Internet.

It Takes a Team to Create a Book

The Tini Sisters weave fun-filled, rhythmic tales that engage and captivate the imagination of children everywhere.

Mair Tini Luchetti is an award-winning poet, certified reading specialist and kindergarten teacher.

Mariellen Tini Sluko is an elementary-school principal.

They each have a Master of Science in the field of education.

Ann Marie Tini is co-founder and president of Atori Publishing. Together with her sister Mair, she assembled an innovative team and began a three-year creative venture, including editing, art direction and design, in order to bring the Letter-Sound™ ♦ Listen and Retell™ Adventure series to life.

Erin Marie Mauterer is an acclaimed children's book illustrator. She has illustrated many picture books and loves splashing them with breath-taking detail. That's the beauty of Erin's art – there is always something more to see.

Carol Ladd is a talented publication designer with over 20 years of experience. One of the most amazing things about the work she has done with this book is that not everything she has created is visible at first glance!